Ducks in Trouble

D1329091

Written and illustrated by
· PATRICE AGGS ·

THE O'BRIEN PRESS
DUBLIN

This edition first published 2009 by The O'Brien Press Ltd,
12 Terenure Road East, Rathgar, Dublin 6, Ireland.
Tel: +353 1 4923333; Fax: +353 1 4922777
E-mail: books@obrien.ie
Website: www.obrien.ie
Originally published as *Ooh La Booga Bomp* in 2001.
Reprinted 2003.

ISBN: 978-1-84717-154-2

British Library Cataloguing-in-Publication Data
A catalogue record for this title is available from The British Library

3   4   5   6   7   8   9   10
09   10   11   12

The O'Brien Press receives assistance from

the arts
council
schomhairle
ealaíon

Typesetting, editing, layout and design: The O'Brien Press Ltd
Printing: Cox & Wyman Ltd

Can YOU spot the panda
hidden in the story?

'What do you think
of this song?' asked Pintail.
He sang a little tune.

'I made it up,' Pintail said.

'It's good,' said Fantail.
'Can I join in?'

Pintail and Fantail
both began to sing.

Down by the pond,
Sploosh and Duckbrain
heard them.
'What a nice song,'
said Sploosh.
'I like it too,' said Duckbrain.

'Pintail made it up,'
said Fantail.
'Why don't you join in?'

'It has words,' said Pintail.

'Cool!' said Sploosh
and Duckbrain.

They began to sing, too.

Up by the duck house,
Goose was trying to rest.
He heard the ducks' song.
'What's that noise?'
Goose honked.

'**Goose**!' shouted Duckbrain.
'Come down and listen.
Pintail has made up a tune.
We are all singing it.'

'You can join in,'
shouted Fantail.

Goose did not come down.
'I can hear it very well
up here,' he said.

'It's very good,' said Sploosh.
'It's **very loud**,' said Goose.
'I'm trying to rest.'

The ducks liked their song.

Sploosh found
a bit of barbed wire.
When Duckbrain
yanked the wire,
it made a cool sound.
Boing! **Boing**!

Then Duckbrain found
a stick and a pan.
When Sploosh hit the pan,
it made a sound like a drum.
Bang! **Bang**!

'Hey! I like that!' said Pintail.
'You guys can be the band.
What a song!'

'What a racket!'
grumbled Goose.
He gave up trying to rest.
He went down to the pond.

'You ducks are making
too much noise,'
said Goose.

'It's late,' he said.
'Everyone is trying to rest.
You'll wake up the farmer
with your singing
and banging.'

JF/2241770

'But it's a good song!'
shouted Pintail.
'You should join in!'

Sploosh banged the pan harder.
Duckbrain pulled harder
on the wire.
Goose left.

They all sang
much louder than before.

'Don't worry about
the farmer,' they sang.
'We won't wake anyone up.'

But they did wake
someone up.

Fox sat up.
'What's that noise?' he asked.

The moon shone.
Fox could see some ducks
singing and banging.
'**Yum**,' said Fox.
Nobody saw him.

'Trumpets!' quacked Fantail.
'That's what this song needs!
We need some trumpets!'

Pintail ran to get
some old flowerpots.
They were great
for the trumpets.

The ducks' song
was getting better.
But it was also getting **louder**.

'Hmm,' said Fox.
'I might creep a little closer.
They're making so much noise
they won't hear me.'

'Dancing!' shouted Sploosh.
'We need a tap dance!'
He got some tiles
from the farmer's shed.
He clapped them together.
They made a noise
just like tap dancing.

CLACK!

CLATTER!

'Look at me!' Sploosh quacked.

He thought his dancing
was good enough
to get on TV.

Pintail and Fantail
and Sploosh and Duckbrain
danced, and sang, and played
their flowerpot trumpets.
They banged their pans
and boinged their barbed wire.

'You don't know
what you're missing, Goose!'
Duckbrain shouted up the hill.
'**Hee, hee, hee!**
This is really fun.'

'**Hee**, **hee**, **hee**!'
laughed Fox.
'Those ducks are so loud!
They can't hear me at all.
I can get up close behind them.
I can easily bite
one of them.'

Goose sat up.

'What are they doing now?'
he groaned.

'Oh no! Tap dancing!

If they wake the farmer–'

Goose stopped.
What was that shape
in the moonlight?

'**Ducks**!' Goose shouted.
'Look behind you!'

But the ducks
could not hear him.
They went on singing
and banging
and boinging
and clacking.

'**Ducks**!'

Goose yelled again.

Goose waved his wings

in the air.

'Look out, ducks!

It's a fox!'

Pintail saw Goose
up by the duck house.
He saw Goose
waving his wings
in the moonlight.

'Come and join the fun, Goose!'
Pintail yelled.

Goose did not stop to think.
He knew what he had to do.
He had to join in.
He had to join in – fast.

Goose ran down to the pond.

He grabbed a flowerpot.

He jumped up and down
on the tiles.

He opened his beak
and **honked** and **honked**.

He made more noise
than all the ducks put together.

'Hey!' shouted Fantail.
'Goose is part of our band
at last!'

'Hey!' shouted Pintail.
'I told you it was fun, Goose!'

'Hey!' shouted Fox.
'What a noise! This is it!
I can jump out
and get them now!'

And he jumped.

'**Hey**!' someone shouted.
It was the farmer!
'**What's that racket**?'

The farmer ran out
his front door.

'Hey!' he shouted again.
'It's a fox!'

Fox yelped.

The ducks all quacked
and yelled.

The tiles and flowerpots
flew into the air.

The farmer ran after Fox
with a big stick.

The farmer chased Fox
far into the woods.
Then he came back
to calm everyone down.

Pintail was still yelling.
Sploosh was still quacking.
Fantail was running around
flapping his wings.
Duckbrain felt sick.

'Oh, thank you for saving us!'
they all said.
The ducks fell in a heap
by the farmer's boots.

'Thank **you**,' said the farmer.
'What clever ducks you are –
making that big noise
to wake me up!
I always thought
ducks were silly.
Now I know better.
You can have
some extra food
in the morning.'

And off he went to his bed.

The ducks looked at each other.
It was very quiet now.

'Well, we *did* wake the farmer,'
said Pintail.

'No, we did not,' said Fantail.
'**Goose** did.
It was all his work.
I feel terrible.'

The ducks marched
up to the duck house.
Goose was trying,
for the fourth time that night,
to get some sleep.

Pintail woke him up.

'Oh no,' said Goose.

'Not again!'

'Goose,' said Pintail.

'We're sorry.'

'We're all sorry,' said Fantail.

'We're *really* sorry,'
said Sploosh.

'Really, **really**–'
began Duckbrain.

Goose waved his wing.
'Stop! That's enough noise,'
he said. 'Go to sleep.
Please!'

And they did.